£7.99

PBR

A Pillar Box Red Publication

we ♥ love you...

Jessie J

A 2013 Annual

Written by Rebecca Bowden
Designed by Duncan Cook Drummond

Contents

Biography | Rise to Fame

Jessie J, born Jessica Ellen Cornish on 27th March 1988 is a UK singer, songwriter and performer who just oozes star quality! She's not your average twenty-something year old pop star, although you'd be forgiven for thinking so at first. Jessie has her own style, attitude and inspirations and knows how to work the music scene.

Jessie J attended Mayfield High School in the London Borough of Redbridge and Colin's Performing Arts School. Aged just 11 years old she was cast in Andrew Lloyd Webber's West End production of *Whistle Down the Wind*. A massive accomplishment and a great career starter!

Jessie has two sisters, who are five and seven years older than her, they were both head girls at school and although Jessie often states that she was "never really that good at anything" at school, we're sure that's just not true! She's amazing.

After suffering a minor stroke when she was younger, Jessie J spent time in and out of hospital. Whilst this may have impaired others, it made Jessie stronger and more determined to succeed. She even managed to draw from some of her experiences to write one of her early songs 'White Room' about a boy on her ward who reportedly later sadly passed away.

Due to having an irregular heart-beat Jessie has to be a lot more sensible with regards to her health than a lot of her fellow pop stars out there! She avoids caffeine, doesn't drink or smoke and is always conscious of the importance of looking after her health.

Jessie is 5ft 9" and doesn't shy away from wearing clothes and styles that accentuate her height. In fact, she positively plays up to it! Often seen in towering heels until an ankle injury in June 2011 saw her rupture tendons in her foot during rehearsals for the Capital Radio Summertime Ball, an injury so serious that it required surgery and means that walking in heels is still painful. Double-Ouch!!

She has a bold, daring and outlandish style which reflects her personality and self-belief. She also famously encourages her fans to be themselves and have confidence in their own abilities.

Jessie J was first signed to Gut Records, but after the company reportedly went bankrupt, she went on to find further success as a songwriter, performer and artist.

Not one to shy away from a challenge, instead of giving up Jessie took herself off to LA under her agents at the time William Morris Agency. She found herself playing in the notorious Viper Room. This was a performance that lead to numerous offers, opening many doors for Jessie J.

Jessie supported Chris Brown on his European tour after being spotted on YouTube by his management, giving her fellow budding musicians hope that these things can and do happen in the music industry!

Her Sony ATV publishing contracts led her to write songs for some of the top US musicians such as Chris Brown, Justin Timberlake, Alicia Keys and Miley Cyrus, the latter of whom optioned 'Party in the USA' written by Jessie, who later stated that she thought the song was much better suited to Miley "To be honest, it was better for her, it's way too straight pop for me. The version I wrote and demo-ed on that day was well ironic."

Jessie J released her first major solo album 'Who You Are' on 25th February 2011. It features the now classic tracks like 'Do it Like a Dude', 'Price Tag' and 'Domino' along with many other mega-hits. Fans immediately embraced the music, rushing out to buy it and sending several tracks soaring to number 1 in the UK charts.

Most recently Jessie has been keeping herself busy with plenty of charity gigs and focusing on her latest project 'The Voice' a UK version of a hit TV show that took the US by storm. The show was generally well received with Jessie's fans being especially happy at the amount of air time Jessie herself received and how amazingly she came across on screen.

Proving her talent and likeability as an artist and a mentor, beyond doubt!

Jessie starred alongside Danny O'Donoghue, will.i.am and Sir Tom Jones as the judging panel and continues to raise her profile worldwide as an influential and positive woman who constantly brings to light new talents and music that are so well loved and respected. Keep it up, Jessie. You rock!

Just Jessie!

Jessie J is well known for her tendency to speak her mind and publicly air her thoughts. That's just one of the reasons why we all love her! Take a look below for some of the best Jessie J quotes, Tweets from her official Twitter account and interview snippets from around the world. Can you remember reading these? We bet there will be a few that will surprise you.

Top Tweets

Jessie is a Twitter regular and can often be found tweeting up a storm to her friends and fans! Here's just a few of her top tweets lately!

We can all moan and complain and feel sad sometimes... But meeting a teenager or someone with cancer puts everything into perspective. Life is so precious and I am so happy I can perform tonight to raise money for TCT. :) – **Jessie Tweeting about her work with Teenage Cancer Trust and her upcoming performance.**
I do my makeup for The Voice for those asking :) – **Tweeting in response to fans who loved her makeup on 'The Voice'.**

12

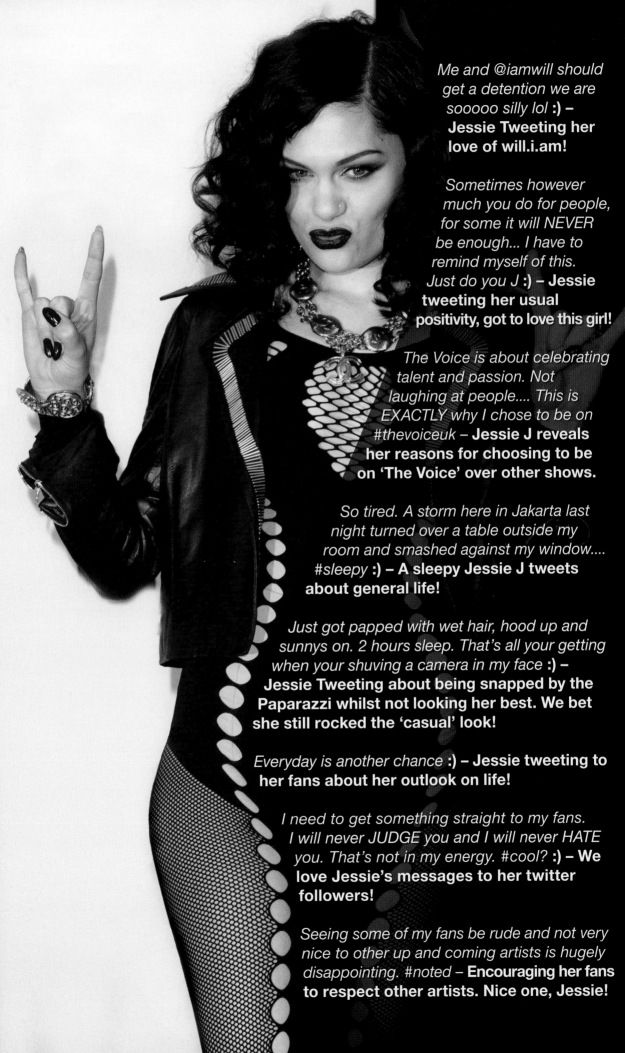

Me and @iamwill should get a detention we are sooooo silly lol :) – **Jessie Tweeting her love of will.i.am!**

Sometimes however much you do for people, for some it will NEVER be enough... I have to remind myself of this. Just do you J :) – **Jessie tweeting her usual positivity, got to love this girl!**

The Voice is about celebrating talent and passion. Not laughing at people.... This is EXACTLY why I chose to be on #thevoiceuk – **Jessie J reveals her reasons for choosing to be on 'The Voice' over other shows.**

So tired. A storm here in Jakarta last night turned over a table outside my room and smashed against my window.... #sleepy :) – **A sleepy Jessie J tweets about general life!**

Just got papped with wet hair, hood up and sunnys on. 2 hours sleep. That's all your getting when your shuving a camera in my face :) – **Jessie Tweeting about being snapped by the Paparazzi whilst not looking her best. We bet she still rocked the 'casual' look!**

Everyday is another chance :) – **Jessie tweeting to her fans about her outlook on life!**

I need to get something straight to my fans. I will never JUDGE you and I will never HATE you. That's not in my energy. #cool? :) – **We love Jessie's messages to her twitter followers!**

Seeing some of my fans be rude and not very nice to other up and coming artists is hugely disappointing. #noted – **Encouraging her fans to respect other artists. Nice one, Jessie!**

13

Quotables

Never one to hold back in interviews, Jessie J is regularly quoted in the media. Her positive attitude and outlandish personality are always the subject of much attention from both fans and tabloids. Here are some of the best Jessie J quotes and snippets!

Speaking at the 2012 Grammy Awards to an E! correspondent on the red carpet Jessie J had the following to say about the shock news of fellow singer Whitney Houston's death. The star expressed her shock and devastation at the news that left everyone at the event, and music fans world-wide so saddened.

"Yesterday was not how I expected it to be. I kind of expected to meet with her and sing with her. But I met her daughter, and I sang for her ... It's still a shock, you know?"

Speaking in a BBC interview about her career, Jessie J says:

"I want young people to know that they can belong - whatever your culture, your religion, your sexuality - that you can live life how you want to live it and feel comfortable how you are."

She adds:

"I think it's really hard to be confident as yourself sometimes, and I think it's important for young people to know that."

"I think that's why my music uplifts people so much because they can see that I'm a normal chick who just wants to bring some goodness to the world."

Jessie J
Factfile!

Ever wanted to find out the facts about your favourite pop star all in one place? Then look no further because here's a handy little Jessie J fact file for you to refer to!

STAGE NAME: Jessie J

BIRTH NAME: Jessica Ellen Cornish

D.O.B: 27/03/1988

HEIGHT: 5ft 9"

LIKES: Positivity, Self-Belief, Honesty, Fashion and Super high heels!

Dislikes: Bullying and Mean or Hurtful Behaviour.

Fears: Heights, Enclosed Spaces.

Interesting Facts

When Jessie J penned the hit record 'Do it Like a Dude' she initially had super-sell-out artist Rihanna in mind, but it was none other than Justin Timberlake who reportedly urged Jessie to keep the track for herself. She is quoted as telling reporters "He was like: 'No, keep it for yourself,' and his advice certainly paid off"!

Jessie has a fear of heights and confined spaces. At one gig they decided to do a blackout and Jessie reportedly suffered a panic attack whilst on stage as she couldn't see where she was or what she was supposed to be doing.

Jessie likes to live a 'clean' healthy lifestyle. Due to her heart problems she can't drink, do drugs, smoke or have caffeine.

Dare Jessie – Jessie loves dares and she encourages her fans to dare her to do random tasks via the 'Dare Jessie J' video category on her official website. One of her most odd dares was to eat as many Ferrero Rocher chocolates as possible in two minutes. Randommm!

15

Jessie J and 'The Voice'

Proving that she always likes to get involved with something fresh and fun, Jessie J was one of the first to sign up for the hit new BBC TV Show 'The Voice': the UK show which encourages coaches to choose the artists in their team based on their vocal talents alone was an instant hit with Jessie J fans who loved this outspoken star and her views.

Rather than being overly critical, the coaches give positive comments and constructive advice to those who don't make it through, making it the perfect show for someone like Jessie who believes in the power of self-belief and positivity.

Each coach sits on a rotating chair. They listen to a contestant sing and if they like what they hear, they can press their button to turn around and 'claim' the act for their team. Of course, if more than one coach turns around the decision of which team to join is down to the contestant. This creates much banter between the judges, especially concerning Jessie J and will.i.am! These two have a lot of fun and plenty of natural chemistry.

Jessie and the Judges!

The coaches panel is packed with fellow talented faces from music and showbiz including:

Sir Tom Jones

Legendary Welsh singer who has sold over 100 million records. Tom was immediately drawn to the bigger, bolder voices much like his own and has dished out some great advice.

will.i.am

The mega talented singer, producer and Black Eyed Peas star has been at the forefront of the action. His banter, chats and fun antics with Jessie J always keep fans giggling throughout! They seem to have become great friends despite the rivalry of the show.

Danny O'Donoghue

He's the lead singer of The Script and an all-round talented guy. Danny typically goes for the soulful, distinctive voices and both he and Jessie have a great friendship with lots of chat and banter.

Jessie's VOICE!

Jessie J isn't scared of speaking up and airing her thoughts about the contestants or what she can do to help them if they join her team. Check out some of our favourite Jessie quotes from the series:

To contestant, Toni - *'Your tone is so old school that I feel like you could teach me something'*

To contestant Max - *'I think you're someone very special, what you did with the two songs was very interesting'*

'I'm excited to be a coach, inspiration and mentor and I jumped at the opportunity as it's all about 'The Voice'.

'I'm so sorry to do this on live TV but my mic is not on,' she said. *'I want it to be perfect.'* - Jessie J after her microphone failed to work during a live performance.

'A great thing as an artist is to have such an amazing quality of artists to choose from.' – Jessie upon making her decision to save Becky Hill.

When asked by Capital FM whether she would be returning for a second series of 'The Voice' Jessie J enigmatically replied *'Who knows? I'm going to keep it a mystery.'*

Styling it up!

We all know that Jessie J is one stylish lady; she even does her own makeup for many of The Voice shows! Here's our style roundup of Jessie's time on screen and some of our favourite fashion and beauty looks.

The Hair!

Purple hair - Jessie shows off some stunning purple hair in the first few episodes of the show. With this popular 'dip dyed' style hair-do she fully lives up to her daring, playful nature. Very pretty!

She can later be seen sporting longer, jet black hair in a variety of exciting styles, and even goes 'girly' with shorter, tousled locks in one show! Whatever the hair Jessie is always known for keeping her style firmly in check throughout!

The Makeup

Jessie is known to love doing her own makeup. She reportedly even did some of her own during her time on the show. She goes for bold, dramatic eye shadow, long dark lashes and anything that stands out from the crowd!

Team Jessie!

Jessie J picked some of her favourite vocal performances over the course of the show and as a result bagged some of the top performers to join her team! Team Jessie was hot, hot, hot!

Some of the competition during the course of each of the audition rounds, the battle rounds and the live shows was astounding and prove that Jessie J is more than just a great singer herself; she also has an unbeatable ear for superb talent spotting!

Spot the Difference

Can you spot eight differences in the pictures above?

Find the answers on page 61.

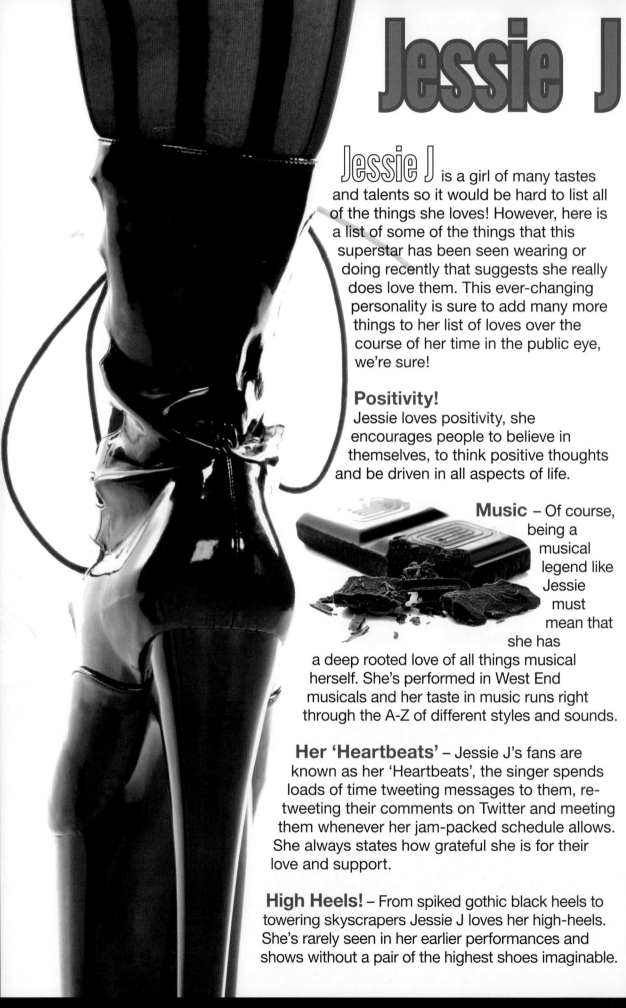

Jessie J

Jessie J is a girl of many tastes and talents so it would be hard to list all of the things she loves! However, here is a list of some of the things that this superstar has been seen wearing or doing recently that suggests she really does love them. This ever-changing personality is sure to add many more things to her list of loves over the course of her time in the public eye, we're sure!

Positivity!

Jessie loves positivity, she encourages people to believe in themselves, to think positive thoughts and be driven in all aspects of life.

Music – Of course, being a musical legend like Jessie must mean that she has a deep rooted love of all things musical herself. She's performed in West End musicals and her taste in music runs right through the A-Z of different styles and sounds.

Her 'Heartbeats' – Jessie J's fans are known as her 'Heartbeats', the singer spends loads of time tweeting messages to them, re-tweeting their comments on Twitter and meeting them whenever her jam-packed schedule allows. She always states how grateful she is for their love and support.

High Heels! – From spiked gothic black heels to towering skyscrapers Jessie J loves her high-heels. She's rarely seen in her earlier performances and shows without a pair of the highest shoes imaginable.

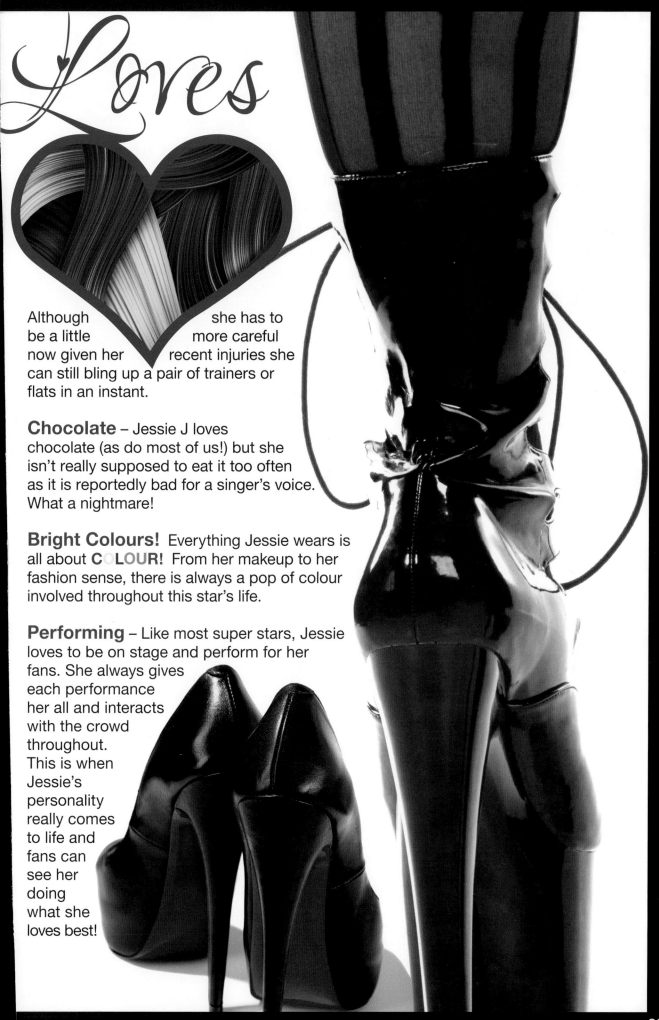

Loves

Although she has to be a little more careful now given her recent injuries she can still bling up a pair of trainers or flats in an instant.

Chocolate – Jessie J loves chocolate (as do most of us!) but she isn't really supposed to eat it too often as it is reportedly bad for a singer's voice. What a nightmare!

Bright Colours! Everything Jessie wears is all about **COLOUR!** From her makeup to her fashion sense, there is always a pop of colour involved throughout this star's life.

Performing – Like most super stars, Jessie loves to be on stage and perform for her fans. She always gives each performance her all and interacts with the crowd throughout. This is when Jessie's personality really comes to life and fans can see her doing what she loves best!

Jessie J Live on Stage!

Here's Jessie J doing what she does best; performing live on stage! Keep reading for all of the best on stage images of this super talented star.

Jessie J rehearses for her performance in Cannes. Before getting ready to mingle with the rich and famous and perform tracks including 'Price Tag', she's seen sporting a casual outfit as she soaks up the electric atmosphere!

Still nursing an injured leg, Jessie performs at V Festival 2011 and wears one of her most colourful outfits yet! Purple hair and a rainbow coloured bodysuit complete the extreme style that this pop superstar is famous for.

Performing live on stage at Big Chill 2011, Jessie rocks some bright purple hair and takes her rightful place on an extravagant throne whilst singing to thousands of fans! Loving that leopard print, Jessie!

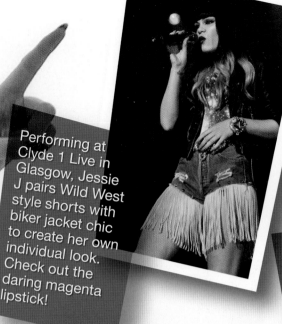

Performing at Clyde 1 Live in Glasgow, Jessie J pairs Wild West style shorts with biker jacket chic to create her own individual look. Check out the daring magenta lipstick!

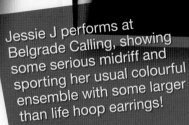

Jessie J performs at Belgrade Calling, showing some serious midriff and sporting her usual colourful ensemble with some larger than life hoop earrings!

Seen again at Belgrade Calling, Jessie casually drapes herself over the stage edge to get up close and personal serenading her fans.

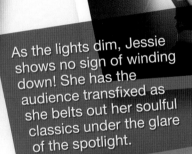

As the lights dim, Jessie shows no sign of winding down! She has the audience transfixed as she belts out her soulful classics under the glare of the spotlight.

The fans go wild for Jessie J as she shows her ability to rock a crowd of varied ages.

Jessie J performs live on stage at Glastonbury Festival in 2011. Seen once again on a huge golden throne, she treats fans to a right royal performance of her hit tracks whilst nursing a painful leg injury.

WORDSEARCH

Can you find the following Jessie J related
words hidden in the wordsearch below?
If you get stuck you can find
the answers at the back!

```
C I H Y Q E S R O M P N F Y F
N S B E L I U I L P O M T M M
C K H L A V E H N P F I P K M
N A E L L R U Z N G L R O Y B
H N N X X Z T D J A E W S R F
M U S I C A L B U G P R I J H
I N D E P E N D E N T T T S D
G V G P H G I R E A A Z I X O
Q X A M H V A F I W T N V J M
W K E Z I R Y T A A R S I E I
E F K D U W G R E O A W T I N
B R N T U B D O C C A Q Y S O
X I E C I O V E H T I H B S B
L I E H H R T A I T J R A E W
N X D S S N U I G V I Q P J F
```

Ellen
The Voice
Price Tag
Jessie J
Singer
Heartbeats
Brit Award

Individuality
Domino
Cornish
Independent
Musical
Positivity

Find the answers on page 60.

Famous Friends!

Here are just a few of Jessie J's famous friends that she's been raving about or spotted out and about with over the course of her career.

will.i.am

Jessie and will.i.am worked together on the popular TV show 'The Voice UK' they instantly seemed to hit it off and despite their constant silly antics, poking fun at one another on stage it genuinely looks as though the pair have a lot of respect for each other going on there!

Tulisa Contostavlos

Jessie J helped Tulisa make her tough decisions over which acts to send through during X Factor 2011. The star flew out to help her good pal Tulisa with this hard decision in the 'judges' houses' round of the hit TV show. Since then the pair have remained close. They regularly tweet and Jessie was one of the first to offer her friend support when recent private videos of the X Factor judge were leaked on to the internet.

Tinie Tempah

They have worked together at various events including the Teenage Cancer Trust concerts, but these two stars have a lot of time for each other and are frequently seen out and about even when they aren't working. There were even rumours that the two were dating after a series of paparazzi shots of them together emerged. Regardless of whether they are anything more than just friends, we think that they make a great team vocally and they look like they get on amazingly well.

Jessie J is very well liked by her fans and by many of the celebrities and musical stars of the world. She has earned the mark of a respected artist in a wide variety of different social circles and is friends with some of the hottest stars.

Adele

Jessie J and Adele know one another from their school days. They attended the London BRIT school together and have briefly kept in touch since. Adele was quoted in The Daily Record as saying of Jessie: *"Jessie J and I went to the same school together. She was in a different class to me"* Adele also added: *"I think her voice is illegal. The things she can do with her voice are criminal."* *"I haven't heard many songs but I have seen acoustic performances online and she is like an acrobat or magician with her voice."*

Justin Timberlake

Justin Timberlake was reportedly the one who persuaded Jessie J to keep 'Do it Like a Dude' for herself instead of giving it to Rihanna! That's gotta be great grounds for a friendship, given how well the track did for Jessie! Plus, who wouldn't want to be friends with the gorgeous Justin?!

Ellie Goulding

"I'm really close with Ellie Goulding. She keeps me sane as she's one of the people who can understand what my life is like." Jessie explained to *Cosmopolitan* as she talked about her most trusted friends and family.

Jessie J

Star Sign Feature

Jessie J's star sign is Aries. Here are some facts and info about your favourite singer's star sign and what is often said the Aries characteristics represent.

Aries Characteristics:

Common characteristics of Aries personalities often include the following. Do you think these relate to Jessie in any way?

Traits: Assertive, Energetic, Adventurous, Dynamic, Impulsive.

Element: Fire

Colours: Bright Red, Scarlet

Aries Animal: The Ram represents Aries.

Birthstone: Diamond

Ruling Planet: Mars

Most compatible with: Other Aries, Leo and Sagittarius.

You could definitely interpret some of these things as fitting Jessie J's personality. The fiery and daring personality and sense of style certainly seems to fit the bill from where we're sitting!

Perhaps there might be some fellow celebs out there with compatible star signs for Jessie to connect with. Only time will tell!

Awards

Jessie J is no stranger to being nominated for awards or winning awards now you mention it! She is one of the most talked about women in music right now and here's just a few of the awards that she has won!

2010
BBC Sound of 2011 Award

2011
Brit Award – Critics' Choice

2011
Jessie stormed the
BT Digital Music Awards
when she won:
Best Newcomer
Best Female Artist
Best Song (Price Tag)

2011
Capital FM Awards
Best Role Model in Pop

2011
Glamour Awards
Woman of Tomorrow Award

2011
Harper's Bazaar Woman of the Year Awards
Breakthrough of the Year Award

2011
She also sensationally stormed the

MOBO Awards

when she won the following:

Best Newcomer
Best UK Act
Best Album (Who You Are)
Best Song "Do It Like a Dude"

2011
Pop Crush Music Awards
Best New Artist

2011
Q Awards
Do it like a Dude – Best Video

2011
Urban Music Awards
Best Female Artist

2011
Virgin Media Awards
Best Newcomer

2012
Silver Clef Awards
Royal Albert Hall Best British Act

There are sure to be **MANY** more prestigious awards to come in the following years for this seriously talented singer!

Charity Work

As with most pop stars, Jessie J likes to do her best to give back something to charities and worthy causes. She has donated much of her time and money to lots of worthwhile events and causes but here are just a few of the things she's been reported to have gotten involved with during her career to help raise money for charities.

Teenage Cancer Trust

Stars from the world of rock, pop and comedy including Florence + The Machines, Jessie J, Example, and Jason Manford, took to the stage of London's Royal Albert Hall between 30th March and 3rd April 2012 to raise money for the Teenage Cancer Trust.

Appearing on each night at London's Royal Albert Hall was Jessie J and these other amazing acts who all gave up their time to support a very worthy cause:

Friday 30 March - Example

Saturday 31 March - Pulp

Sunday 1 April - Jessie J

Monday 2 April - Jason Manford hosted an evening of comedy

Tuesday 3 April - Florence & The Machine

VH1 Save the Music Foundation

Jessie J was kind enough to add her autograph to a Raymond Weil Freelancer Crazy Time watch, in chartreuse green with a diamond studded dial and bezel. This was signed and kissed during the 2012 ELLE Women in Music event by multi-platinum international artist Jessie J, singer/songwriter Ellie Goulding, Danish singer Oh Land, Pussycat Dolls Nicole Scherzinger, songwriter Dianne Warren, actor/singer Diego Boneta, Editor-in-Chief of ELLE magazine, Robbie Meyers and many more.

To enter, fans could place their bids on the Raymond Weil Facebook page. The retail value of the watch was $5,750.

Donating to Charity Shops and the Homeless

Jessie J recently told The Sun newspaper: "I get given a lot of clothes and

I don't always like them so I give them to homeless people or to local charity shops. There are some cool homeless people who are kitted out around my area now. The charity shop near where I live has loads of my clothes in the window. We walked past and all my friends were liking these gold shoes and I screamed, well, they are mine".

Children's Hospice Association Scotland (Chas)

Jessie J, Jason Derulo and the Sugababes all donated unique personal artwork to an auction in aid of a Scottish children's hospice charity.

Singers Will Young and Pixie Lott as well as British boy bands One Direction, JLS and The Wanted also contributed doodles to be sold off to raise cash for the Children's Hospice Association Scotland (Chas).

Jessie J crafted a self-portrait and kissed the paper to leave a lipstick mark on the face and Jason Derulo shared a picture of himself as a microphone with a giant afro. Will Young sketched a cartoon chicken and Pixie Lott kept it traditional by painting the Scottish countryside alongside her autograph.

The signed images were auctioned off at a Real Radio charity event on 14 April 2012.

There are also of course those rumours of Jessie J still thinking about shaving her hair off for charity. Do we think she'll do it?! If anyone is brave enough it is certainly her!

35

Jessie J – Just do YOU

Jessie J always urges her fans to 'just do you' a statement which is not only a lyric from her hit song 'Mamma Knows Best' but that also once again highlights her care for her fans and her belief that you should always stay true to who you are and have confidence in yourself.

Here are some ways that we think you can be amazing, just by being YOU!

Believe in yourself!

Believing in yourself is one of the key things to remember if you want to succeed in anything life throws your way! We all have those special qualities that make us unique and with a little bit of self-belief anything really is possible. Just look at how far Jessie has come. No matter how shy you are, just remember that you will never know if you don't dare to try!

Embrace your own style!

We all have our own individual style. Some of the things that look amazing on one person may not look so great on another. Find a style that you are comfortable in and don't be afraid to wear it! Jessie rocks her own unique and daring sense of style because it is probably what she feels happiest in. You can do the same simply by thinking about the kind of looks you love and what suits you best. We all come in different shapes and sizes and we are ALL beautiful inside and out, our clothing doesn't have to define us. Just be yourself!

Stand up for what you believe in!

Your opinion matters. It also helps shape who you are and who you will become. Don't be afraid to have your own opinion, even if it is different from your best-friends. Stand up for what you believe is right and don't let anyone drag you down.

Look for the positive!

Jessie J has been through her fair share of ups and downs in her life. She's battled through various heart and health problems and has had to change her life in ways that many teenagers might have found frustrating. No matter what, Jessie always took a negative and turned it into a positive, focusing on her career and her goals despite her health problems and encourages her fans to be as positive as they can. Her messages and tweets never single people out; she doesn't like to see her fans being unkind and hurtful and prefers to be upbeat and fun, tackling things head on. What a great attitude to life!

Be amazing, be **YOU!**

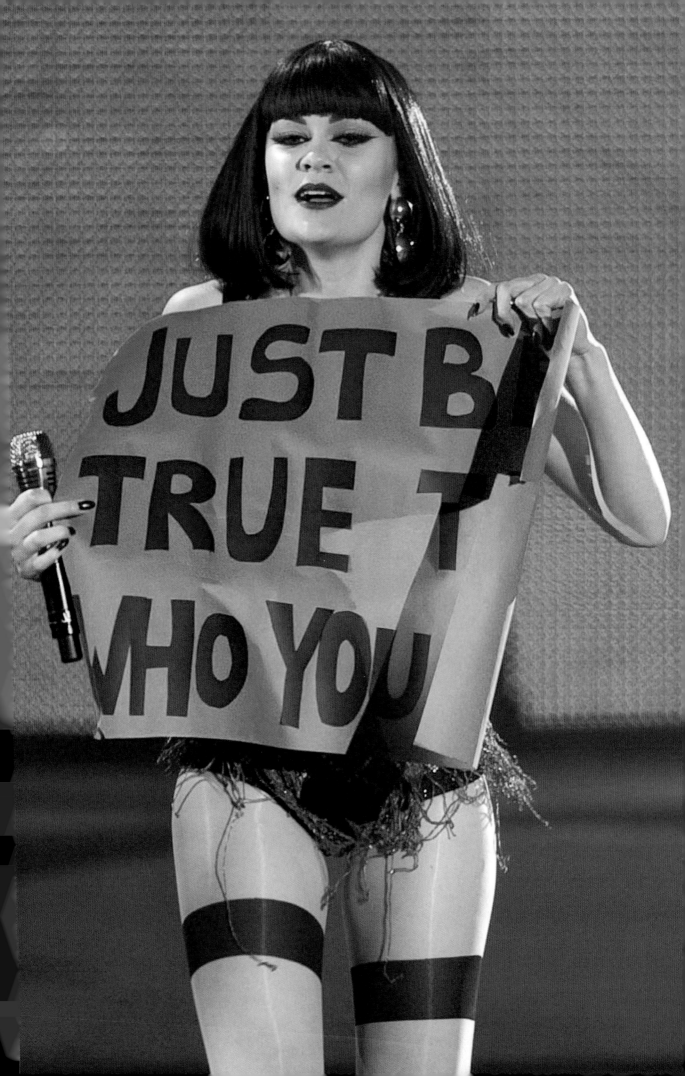

Jessie J FashionFOCUS!

Jessie J has a look and style that is all her own. She stands out from the crowds with her towering frame and stunning fashion sense that shows off her love of bold and exciting colours. She is far from a shy and retiring wallflower and her fashion sense reflects this. Here are some of Jessie's most documented fashion faves!

Hair

Jessie is usually seen with her trademark jet black hair in a blunt cut bob which fans are so familiar with. However she does like to experiment with her hairstyles and we have seen her embrace the dip dye hair

trend for a while now. She's gone from long, luscious locks with dip dyed purple ends one day and dip dyed blonde ends the next! She also briefly had flame red and rainbow colours running through her hair! This girl is not afraid to embrace her own individuality!

She's rocked an all-out bright purple bob, slicked back ponytails and a mass of wavy curls, managing to look boldly beautiful with every different style.

Lips

Jessie loves bright colours on her lips. Her trademark lipstick is probably a good quality bright, blood red but she's also prone to wearing bright pink, magenta, purple and even a union jack theme painted on her pout for one occasion! Of course, like the rest of us she's also spotted out and about just wearing a good old fashioned nude lipstick with a slick of gloss. Even this fun loving lady has to tone it down sometimes!

Clothing

Jessie is well known for her outlandish outfits, especially whilst performing. She loves towering high heels (although she has revealed that since her foot injury these aren't as easy to wear as they used

to be!) and daring outfits.
She loves leotards, bodysuits, cat-suits and anything that shows off those perfect pins of hers! Teamed with boots or some sassy heels she's never at risk of blending in to the background. Colourful prints, metallic-look jackets and footwear also play a regular part in Jessie J's wardrobe regulars.

Jewellery

Jessie J doesn't do understated when it comes to jewellery and accessories. She keeps it 'bling' with bold and chunky necklaces, rings and seems to favour gold over silver any day of the week! She likes statement pieces and unusual items and we think that they represent her personality perfectly.

All in all, Jessie J is one well-dressed diva! Her look is always on-trend and up to date with her own quirky slant. Perfect!

41

Jessie J Mega Quiz

Do you consider yourself a huge Jessie J fan? Take our mega-quiz and see how many of the answers you get right. Don't worry if you get stumped, you can find the answers at the back, but no cheating!

Ok, let's start with an easy one...

1. What is Jessie J's real name?

2. Which of these movies has a Jessie J track in it?

    Easy A
    The Notebook
    Titanic

3. Where is Jessie from?

4. What did Jessie once say she planned to do to her hair for charity in 2012?

5. What are Jessie's two sisters called?

6. Can you name Jessie J's first single?

7. What was Jessie diagnosed with at age 11?

8. Can you name the song that Jessie J wrote for Miley Cyrus?

9. What are Jessie J fans known as?

10. Which West End production was Jessie J cast in?

11. How did Jessie J break her ankle at the Summertime Ball?

12. What was one of the main reasons other kids used to bully Jessie J when she was younger and on medication?

13. When is Jessie's birthday?

14. Which American artist features on the track "Price Tag"?

15. At what age did Jessie suffer her stroke?

16. Which girl group did Jessie used to be part of?

17. What is Jessie J's debut album called?

18. What was Jessie J's mum's job?

19. What was Jessie J's dad's job?

How many did you get right? Are you a bona fide natural Jessie J know-it-all, or do you need to work on your knowledge of all things Jessie J related? Hopefully you had fun either way.

Find the answers on page 61.

Spot the Difference

Can you spot eight differences in the pictures above?

Find the answers on page 61.

45

Jessie J LyricsQuiz!

Are you a top Jessie J fan? Can you spot which lyrics are from which Jessie J track? Here's a quiz to put your knowledge to the test and see just how much attention you pay to those amazing tunes!

1. Stomp stomp, I've arrived
   Drop the beat, nasty face
   Why ya lookin' at me?

2. Tilt my head and feel the tears roll down. Cause my eyes can't see in the dark, I feel numb, broken, and so so scared. (mmm) I don't wanna be here anymore, I wanna be somewhere else, Roaming free, like I used to be.

3. Why is everybody so obsessed? Money can't buy us happiness Can we all slow down and enjoy right now Guarantee we'll be feelin All right.

4. I can taste the tension like a cloud of smoke in the air Now I'm breathing like I'm running cause you're taking me there. Don't you know...you spin me out of control....

5. Why can't you see the truth when is right in front of you You don't love me anymore so I guess way through...

Answers on page 61.

Look to the Future

The future holds so much for Jessie J! She's still in the early days of her career and look how far she's already come. This is one star that is undoubtedly destined for great things and everyone is speculating just where they might lead.

Here are some of the top things that could happen to Jessie J in the future if she plays her cards right. We can't wait to see if any of these come true. What would your own Jessie J future predictions be?

Release her own clothing line

This is one thing that just HAS to happen eventually. Jessie is so keen to play around with different styles, fashion trends and hot looks that she would make a great designer! Who knows,

maybe in the next few years she might have her own fashion label or a hot designer collection on her hands. That's if she has time with all of the amazing music she makes!

Duet with more celebs

Ok so Jessie J has already sung with her fair share of celebrities and well-known names but who might she hook up with musically in the future? There are always bright and talented new stars arising as well as some all-time classics. Maybe a duet with her fellow 'The Voice UK' coach Sir Tom Jones might happen as we already know they get on incredibly well and both have super powerful voices? Only time will tell!

Raise millions for charity

Jessie J is one of the top UK stars who always go the extra mile for charity. If she continues this way there must be millions of charities that she could continue to use her talents to help raise money for. This is something that will almost definitely happen, knowing how committed to helping others less fortunate than herself Jessie already is.

Start her own record label

Jessie loves encouraging new and rising talent. Maybe one day she might start her own record label and mentor those who she thinks can go far? If will.i.am can do it, we're sure that one day Jessie can too!

Meet the love of her life

Will Jessie J fall in love and live happily ever after? She's been linked to a few fellow singers so who knows, maybe in the not so distant future she will find her soul-mate and settle down. Well, as much as anyone could ever tame the wild child that is Jessie J of course!

Just keep doing 'Jessie'

One thing is for certain, if there is one star who certainly won't lose sight of herself along the way it is Jessie J. Wherever the future takes her and whatever it may hold, she will continue to do what she loves and embrace the things that make her and the army of fans who surround her happy. That's why we love her!

Jessie News!!

Jessie J is one busy lady, but here are just a few of the things that she's been doing in more recent months. Despite some run-ins with fatigue bugs and other illness she's managed to cram her schedule full of gigs, appearances and updates.

The Voice

Jessie Jessie J has confirmed that she will be returning as a coach on the BBC talent show *The Voice*.

The singer tweeted:
"The Voice UK Series 2... Are you ready?! I AM ;)"

Since the show ended earlier this year, there had been rumours that Jessie J would not be rejoining the panel.

However her second tweet made it clear she would be part of the second series.

"I WILL be a coach on the 2nd series of The Voice UK!

"I'm B B B BACK! As I have always said. Unless you hear it from me – Don't always believe what you read! Can't wait!"

Courtesy of BBC Radio 1 Newsbeat

Olympics 2012

Jessie J made us all proud with her excellent performance at the London 2012 Olympic Games Closing Ceremony.

itunes Festival 2012

Jessie J took to the stage for the itunes festival in 2012 alongside other top artists such as Usher, Pink, David Guetta, Plan B, One Direction, Ed Sheeran, Biffy Clyro and Noel Gallagher's High Flying Birds.

There were around 60 artists playing across 30 nights at the Roundhouse in Camden, London throughout September 2012 and Jessie's performance only added to the excitement of such a high profile event, which allowed hundreds of thousands of music fans the opportunity to see their idols perform up close and personal.

Overcoming Illness

Jessie J overcame illness during July of 2012 to perform at Ibiza's Eden and Mallorca's BCM nightclubs in Spain. After having to cancel a few gigs previously but receiving the all clear from doctors, a very happy Jessie J tweeted *"I'm so pleased that I'm able to play my gigs to my fans tomorrow, watch out @myibizalive & @mymallorcalive I'm coming to get'cha!! Boooooom!!"*

Jay James Picton sings Jessie J's Praises!

It's no secret that Jessie J has a lot of supporters and fans in the entertainment industry. The latest to speak out about his thoughts on the star was singer Jay James Picton who recently supported Jessie on tour in 2012. He said:

"She's amazing. I'm very rarely complementary towards certain artists, but Jessie is certainly an artist to be proud of with what the UK brings out."

"Everything that she does is 1000 per cent who she is. When you see her on stage, she is herself. She's a real inspiration."

The Jessie J Effect!

Jessie J has a profound effect on some of the lives of her biggest fans. She encourages them and tries her best to be honest and up front about issues and topics that come up. In return they are always supportive and loyal to this rising UK superstar.

Jessie has named her fans 'Heartbeats' and regularly mentions them on social media website Twitter and retweets their messages of support. She takes to her Twitter, Facebook and official website to address her fans regularly and keep them in the loop regarding upcoming gigs; her latest gossip and goings on, making them feel like they too are an important part of her life. She produces and releases intimate and in-depth videos of her general life and life on the music scene on her official website and invites fans to get involved. Unlike some musicians, she certainly isn't afraid to embrace her fame and doesn't seem to be overwhelmed by the support from her millions of fans worldwide.

Jessie J has an upbeat and caring personality and public persona that certainly rubs off on her fans. They are always encouraged to stand up for themselves and have a great sense of self belief as Jessie's way of thinking seems to be that nothing is impossible if you want it badly enough. She rarely has time to slate or berate other musicians or celebs and that is one of the things that helps make her so unique and refreshing in the music industry today.

The media have always been relatively kind to Jessie where coverage is concerned, she gets the occasional bad review or some stick for something she's done but they are definitely more 'on side' than 'off' in most cases. Her laid back attitude and the fact that she rarely appears to let what the press say get to her probably has something to do with this!

Loyal fans will undoubtedly continue to support Jessie J in all of her further ventures as her unrelenting passion for music and people continue to show themselves. She fights for what she wants and isn't afraid to stand up and say what she believes in. That's what makes Jessie J the hottest property in the music scene right now and those are just some of the reasons why her fans love her and why she has such an amazing effect on so many of them. Maybe you can come up with your own reasons why you agree that Jessie J is your favourite star of the moment?

Of course, like any star, Jessie J has been caught having the odd few bad hair days, wardrobe malfunctions and all of the usual paparazzi shots that come with being famous but none of them seem to halt this daring star's sense of determination and strength.

UK Fans and media have supported Jessie J and her move to prime time live TV in the BBC show 'The Voice' and her attitude and supportive nature on this show has only gone to further prove her genuine, kind-hearted nature and her love of music in various different styles and forms.

A-Z of Jessie J

A – is for **ALBUMS** – Jessie makes the best!

B – is for **BLING** Jessie wears loads of bling on her super cool accessories.

C – is for **CONFIDENCE** because Jessie J is one confident lady!

D – is for **DARING** clothes and attitude!

E – is for **ENCOURAGEMENT** as she's forever encouraging the acts on 'The Voice UK', even those who don't make it through.

F – is for **FANS!** Jessie loves her fans and all that they represent.

G – is for **GIRL POWER!**

H – is for **HEALTHY** as Jessie tries to live a healthy lifestyle.

I – is for **ILLNESS** – Jessie has overcome many illnesses in her life and doesn't let it hold her back.

J – is for **JUST DO YOU** Jessie's message to fans.

K – is for **KIND**. She's kind and thoughtful to others.

L – is for **LOVE**

M – is for **MIC** bringing Jessie's amazing voice to you loud and clear!

N – is for **NICE** – Fans hail her as one of the nicest female singers on the music scene today.

O – is for **ORIGINALITY**

P – is for **PASSION** – Jessie has a real passion for her music and being her own person.

Q – is for **QUEEN OF HEARTS** – Jessie has a big heart and always makes time for those she cares about.

R – is for **RECORDING ARTIST** – Jessie J records the BEST tracks!

S – is for **SHOES** – Jessie always wears the coolest footwear.

T – is for **TWITTER** as Jessie is always tweeting!

U – is for **UNDERSTANDING!** She always tries to see other's point of view as well as her own.

V – is for **VAMP!** Jessie loves to vamp it up with dramatic dark eyes, black hair and blood red lips.

W – is for **will.i.am** – friend and fellow coach on "The Voice UK. "

X – is for **X FACTOR** – Jessie reportedly turned down Simon Cowell's advances to try and lure her to his TV show.

Y – is for **YOUTH** – Jessie reaches out and supports her younger fans.

Z – is for **ZAPPED** as Jessie has definitely zapped us all with her amazing vocals and now we can't get her songs out of our heads!

QUIZ ANSWERS

WORDSEARCH p.27

SPOT THE DIFFERENCE p.21

ULTIMATE JESSIE J QUIZ p.42

1. Jessica Ellen Cornish
2. Easy A
3. Essex
4. She said she would consider shaving it all off
5. Hannah & Rachel
6. Do it Like a Dude
7. An irregular heartbeat
8. Party in the USA
9. Heartbeats
10. Whistle Down the Wind
11. She fell off her podium whilst rehearsing
12. Because tablets to help her heart condition turned her skin green
13. 27th March 1988
14. B.o.B
15. 18
16. Soul Deep
17. Who You Are
18. She was once a nursery school teacher
19. He was once a social worker

SPOT THE DIFFERENCE p.45

LYRICS QUIZ p.48

1. Do it like a Dude
2. Big White Room
3. Price Tag
4. Domino
5. Run Baby

Where's Jessie?